# Rainbow Kittens

Written by V.C. Graham
Illustrated by Lisa Alderson

7373 North Cicero Avenue
Lincolnwood, Illinois 60712

Ground Floor, 59 Gloucester Place
London W1U 8JJ

Permission is never granted for commercial purposes.

Customer Service: 1-800-595-8484 or customer_service@pilbooks.com

**www.pilbooks.com**

p i kids is a trademark of Publications International, Ltd., and is registered in the United States.

8 7 6 5 4 3 2 1

ISBN-13: 978-1-4508-2991-5
ISBN-10: 1-4508-2991-0

One shimmery, summery morning,
seven very special kittens were born.

Mama cat named the first kitten Ruby.

Next came Punkin, because he was roly-poly.

She named the third kitten Daisy.
Can you guess why?

Fourth was Lucky, as in "lucky clover."

Bluebelle's brothers and sisters
call her Belle, for short.

Indigo was between Belle and Violet.

And just because her name is Violet,
everybody thinks she's shy. But she's not!

Ruby and Punkin like to look for things that are red and orange.

Will you help, too?

Daisy and Lucky like to look
for yellows and greens.

What do you see?

Belle is on the hunt for something blue.
She sees it!

Do you see it, too?

Indigo and Violet are almost twins,
so they both prefer to pounce on purples.
Can you point to some pouncy purples?

Mama cat calls all of her kittens. It is time to come fill their tummies and take a nap.

Mama cat loves her rainbow kittens!